Erasmus Jones

History of the Town of Frankfort

Erasmus Jones

History of the Town of Frankfort

ISBN/EAN: 9783337268169

Printed in Europe, USA, Canada, Australia, Japan

Cover: Foto ©Andreas Hilbeck / pixelio.de

More available books at **www.hansebooks.com**

HISTORY

OF THE

Town of Frankfort,

BY

Erasmus Jones.

WINTERPORT:
Advertiser Job Print.
1897.

PREFACE.

This little History, should you term it such, was published by C. R. Lougee, with the kind assistance of Mrs. Charles Abbott, and Mr. E. Ferren Blaisdell. It tells of the old town of Frankfort when first settled and also speaks of olden time people, their customs, with many historical sketches in the days when Winterport and Frankfort were one.

By request of some of the older inhabitants we publish this little book and hope it will be favorably received.

The Blaisdell Homestead, the oldest house in town.
Built in 1785.   (See page 56.)

HISTORY OF FRANKFORT.

In 1766 there were two log houses in what is now Frankfort, (Winterport) one near where the Sampson house now stands(now, in 1896, a house owned by Mrs. Dr. Thayer on the lot) built by John Dunton afterwards occupied by Ephriam Grant and the other on the McGlathry place built by Joshua Ayres, subsequently occupied by John Couillard. There was to be seen at this time, the remains of a battery on high head, now the Tappan lot (T. Cushing lot) supposed to have been built by Baron Castine; a hollow place has marked the spot until within a few years.

In 1772 the first survey was made in this town. A line was then run parallel with the river and one mile back. This line commenced at the Cove and run straight to the Marsh stream, which it hits near the spring beyond the guide post on the road to Campbell's Mills. On this line monuments were erected every fifty rods, dividing it into 100 acre lots; this is still known as the Chadwick line, named from its surveyor, and is the head bound of all the lots on the river within the compass named above. Upon the plan of that survey were put down, besides the houses already mentioned, one on the Low brook lot, occupied by one Low; on the Cain lot now known as the Martin place occupied by Wilson,(now occupied by G. H. Dunton) on the Lombard lot, and one on the

Renny place, occupied by Hatevil Colson.   These were all log houses.

In the year 1779 this river was the scene of one of the most disastrous affairs which darkens the page of our revolutionary history.   The largest and best equipped fleet fitted out in this country during the war, was here completely annihilated.   The enemy having landed a force at Bagaduce, now Castine, and commenced intrenchments there, it being in the jurisdiction of Massachusetts, a fleet was promptly fitted out from Boston consisting of nearly twenty armed vessels, ships, brigs and sloops of war.   One of them, the ship Warren, was furnished by the general government, and was the flag ship of the fleet.   Besides the armed vessels there were about the same number of transports—vessels employed to carry troops and supplies.   The marine and land forces amounted to about 6,000 men.   Gen. Lovell commanded the latter and Com. Salstonstal the fleet.   Upon arriving at Bagaduce some attempts were made to capture the place but nothing effectual done until the enemy had time to hem them in with a more powerful fleet.   The commanders appear to have been very inefficient men, and all that was now thought of was flight.   Two of the vessels in attempting to make their escape round the western end of Long Island were captured by the enemy, the remainder of the fleet retreated up the river, were set on fire by their crews and blown up, or burnt to the water's edge and sunk.   One vessel was sunk opposite Sampson's ledge, she has since been visited by a diving bell and some iron articles brought up.   The flag ship Warren was destroyed at Oak

Point—her decks were strewed with oil and set on fire, soon the magazine was reached and blown to fragments. She contained in part the stores of the fleet, and it is said the shore was strewed with biscuits like flakes of snow. Some of her remains may still be seen imbedded in the mud. The sloops of war Monmouth, Sally and Black Prince, each carrying 20 guns were destroyed at Hampden. The number of vessels in all destroyed between Castine and Bangor was 33. The troops and marines were marched through the wilderness to Fort Halifax on the Kennebec opposite Waterville. The first which went through used a compass and spotted trees as a guide to those who should follow, when they came to Long Pond in Unity they spotted a road on both sides of it, in consequence of which, the second party in following the trail went around the pond two or three times. The men suffered much on the march. Though there was abundance of provision in the fleet, they were not provident enough to take a sufficient supply with them, and before they got through were obliged to resort to Indian cucumbers and the bark of trees for food. They were five days in performing the journey.

The History of Frankfort, from which these sketches are taken, was written for an association of young people called "The Mutual Improvement Society," by Erasmus Archibald Jones, about the year 1844. Mr. Jones was assisted by many of the early settlers whose memories were still fresh with the early scenes herein narrated, particularly Archibald Jones, Esq., and Tisdale Dean, gentlemen who took prominent parts in many of these incidents. Archibald Jones, father of E. A. Jones, came here from Worcester, Mass., in 1802, he was the first lawyer who settled here.   He decided on this place as the probable location of the future city on the Penobscot, from its being the head of winter navigation.   He died February, 1858, aged 81 years.

Capt. Ross, of the ship Monmouth, having had a leg broken at Castine, and being unable to march with his comrades, took up his lodgings at Capt. Ephraim Grant's.   The English surmising he was somewhere on the river, were on the alert for him, when they were known to be near, Capt. Grant, who was a powerful man, took him on his back and carried him up into the valley in the Sampson pasture and hid him in a thicket where he had a bed for him.   He finally made his escape by the British and got home. Capt. Grant, with part of his family, fearing molestation from the enemy, performed the journey to the Kennebec.   When they returned it was in the winter and snow shoes were used, their provisions being hauled on hand sleds.   During their absence, their place had been visited by a privateer, their hay carried off to Bagaduce, and their house converted into barracks.

Provisions were very scarce and high during this period.   Flour was $24 per barrel and meal $4 per bushel.   Some of the inhabitants lived wholly on fish and milk, and what game they killed in the woods. Moose were very plenty.   One man who lived here at that time relates that he has killed seventeen in one spring, and used almost every day to see them when he went up to Oakman hill after his cattle. Other game was very abundant, moose, deer, otters, bears, wolves, martins, foxes and hares. Upon a meadow one mile from this village may still be seen the remains of a beaver dam, by which the meadow was at one time flowed. One old lady used to tell of seeing a hawk flying at this time of scarcity with a fish in his claws. When he was over her head, she raised such a scream as caused him to drop the fish, upon which she made an excellent dinner.

At the time of which we have been treating, there was one house at Hampden, none at Bangor. The settler at Hampden was Col. Gouldthrite, for some time he was the commander of Fort Point. He was a noted Tory, and at the conclusion of the war, in making his escape to the Provinces with a large number of others of like character, was ship wrecked and lost. After peace was concluded, this country began to be settled. Those who had left the river, returned and others came and commenced settlements.

The first frame house erected in Frankfort was in 1781 by one Smith, on what is now the Holmes place near the Steam Mill.

In 1783 the Grant house just back of Capt. John Arey's(afterward Capt. Edwin Littlefield's, which was burnt down) was built, and was standing until within a few years, when it was pulled down. The Grant barn, built the same year, still stands(1844) bearing indubitable signs of age.

The house now owned by E. F. Blaisdell was built in 1785 by his grandfather, Ebenezer Blaisdell.

At this time the nearest physician was Dr. Crawford at Fort Point.

A story is handed down of Col. Gouldthrite, who kept the fort at Fort Point, that at a time when he was preparing for some great feasting occasion, he employed an Indian to kill a moose for him. When the Indian appeared with his game the colonel asked him where he had found "so fat a moose." He replied "It is your horse," but it was thought he was joking, and the supposed moose meat was highly relished. When the colonel came to hunt for his horse, which had been turned out to graze at a distance from home, he was not to be found, and then it was known the Indian had told the truth.

In 1789 the town of Frankfort was incorporated. Previously it had been called Marsh Bay. At the time of its incorporation it included all of Prospect, part of Newburg and most of Hampden. The seat of government was at Sandy Point. Here the town meetings were held and this was the principal place of trade.

At this time, in addition to the settlers already named, Tobias Oakman lived in a house which was afterwards burned, near the site of Tobias O. Thompson's house. Miller Johnson lived in a house between the house now occupied by his son, Thomas Johnson, and the river. Moses Littlefield, a revolutionary soldier, on the Martin place (now G. H. Dunton's)

Judge Goodwin, who was surgeon mate on board the U. S. Ship Warren when she was destroyed, John Bolan, I. Haegan on Atwood place, Kempton on Oak Point, Clark on the Hardy place and Joshua Treat on Treat's Point.

The only horse in town was owned by Parson Carleton, who lived in Goshen. Oxen were more plenty. Everything was drawn on sleds in summer, as well as in winter, as there were no wheels and no roads fit for them. At one time, a party was given by Mr. Treat at the Point, to attend which, ox sleds were called into requisition by the beaux and belles of that day.

Tobias Haley came here in 1791; John McIntire in 1792; about this time Enoch Sampson and Esquire McGlathry came; Sampson built a house still called the Sampson house(now on the lot owned by Mrs. Dr. Thayer;) a wharf which was the first wharf built here, and a store near it in which he traded, a barn on the lot which Mr. H. W. Emerson now occupies, remained a long time in a delapidated condition, affording a night's lodging for some homeless person as "old Clifton," the terror of the school children.

In 1794 Prospect and Hampden were set off. Judge Goodwin was the first Representative to the General Court held in Boston.

In 1802 the Blaisdell house (now occupied by Capt. Dudley) was built and a store near it. A. L. Kelley's house, called the Cox House, which was used as a tavern, the Dutch House, (a cottage opposite what is now N. H. Hubbard's,) a store where the brick school house now stands, (where Nason Brothers' meat market is,) and Hall's store had been built, also a wharf near Hall's store; there are still some remains of this wharf near the outlet of Low's brook.

From 1802 to 1806 there were eleven houses and three stores built, all two story buildings except two —the house where Joseph Robinson lives, (now owned by F. C. Young) which was built by Dr. Peabody, the first physician who lived here; he remained but a few years then removed to Levant. The Freeman house opposite Patrick McShea's. Tisdale Deane's house, first used as a store, was built by Daniel Livermore; he afterwards built Benj. Shaw's house.

Livermore was a passionate tempered man and on being insulted by Capt. Clements he struck him on the head with a billet of wood, which so injured him that his life was despaired of. Livermore, who lived at Monroe at this time, felt very uneasy about it, and on inquiring of a man concerning his state was answered, "Capt. Clements is dead; I have just come from there and assisted in laying him out." Upon hearing this news, Livermore packed up his valuables and fled. He has never returned, though his supposed victim is alive still. Livermore's widow died the present month in Monroe at the advanced age of eighty-nine.

Mrs. Andrews' house built by Simeon Kenney; Mrs. Milliken's (now Benj. Hall's) built by Abel Curtis, who followed the sea; Oliver Couillard's house, built by Reuben Winchell, a mason by trade; John Stokell house; widow Arey's house, built by Esquire Merrill; Deborah Thompson's house, built by a Mr. Cox, who kept tavern in the Kelley house, likewise Wm. Holmes' store, (where Moody's cooper shop now is) which was built and occupied by Thurston and Thorndike, McGlathry's store, occupied by John McGlathry (where F. W. Haley's store now is;) Tisdale Deane's store, (now A. E. Fernald's) was built at this time by Bradshaw Hall, who afterwards removed to Castine and was Register of Deeds At this time, also, Esquire Merrill traded in the store located on the brick school house lot.

In the autumn of 1806, a new store was opened in the building now occupied by John Stokell (since burnt down and rebuilt.) It was the firm of Andrews, Ware & Dean. The trade at that time was almost wholly barter, being an exchange of provisions, West India, English and Domestic goods, of which rum formed a very important article, for oak hogshead and barrel staves, rift clapboards and shingles, spruce knees, cord wood and bark.

An idea of the providence of the country people at that time may be obtained by the following anecdote, related by one of the first traders. He said that a man from Monroe, which was then called Lee, used to bring him corn in the fall to exchange for goods as long as his corn lasted, and, knowing that he would want it all back in the spring, he used to put it by itself, and when the man came to be a purchaser of corn he sold him the same corn for $1.00 per bushel that he had paid him 75c. for. The profit of the transaction to the producer after transporting his corn both ways, with no roads, perhaps it would be difficult to calculate.

The roads here in 1806 were anything but turnpikes judging by a description of them by a gentleman who landed here at that time. He said that on the first day of his arriving he left his horse, which he had brought with him, to himself, and being very busy during the day in landing his effects, did not think of him again until night, when on looking for him he was not to be found. He went in search of him and followed the main road up as far as where James Haley lives, and there the road was so obstructed by pine stumps and roots running across it above the ground he came to the conclusion that no horse could get farther in that direction.

A gentleman who was engaged in trade at that time has given me the prices of some articles in which he dealt.

Such sheetings as now sell from eight to ten cents were then sold at forty or fifty cents per yard; molasses 75 to 87 1-2 cents; Souchong tea $1,00 per lb.; coffee 25 to 30 cents; clear pork 25 cents; ginger 33 1-3 cents; saleratus 30 cents and nutmegs 9 pence (12 1-2 cents) apiece.

He says that Gov. Porter, as he is familiarly called, kept an old horse with which he hauled or twitched out spruce knees, which he exchanged for goods as his necessities demanded, and he had done it so repeatedly that the old horse learned the business as well as his master and frequently came alone and stopped in front of his store with his load.

At this period the only school house was at the Marsh; the school in this village was kept in part of A. L. Kelley's house.

There was occasionally preaching by a missionary in private houses. Father Sawyer sometimes preached; there were also some native preachers; sometimes barns were converted into meeting houses for a Sabbath. Elder Adam Grant was one of the native preachers who sometimes held forth in the Sampson barn. What the effect of his preaching was upon his human auditors has not been handed down, but on one occasion he halooed so loud that he terrified a calf to that degree that he jumped out of the barn window, took to the woods, and was not recovered for a week.

At this time Bangor was not essentially larger than Frankfort, and contained but three or four stores. Bucksport had somewhat the start of it. Belfast was about equal to Bucksport. Castine was the principal place of trade on the river. It was not until about the year 1807 that an ox wagon was imported into town; previous to that time there had never been any wheels seen here. When the snow went off in the spring the country people brought their lumber to market on a kind of vehicle that has entirely disappeared, and therefore will need a description. It consisted of two long poles with rungs like a ladder, an open space being left at one end for the horse, the other dragging on the ground. The forward end of

the poles entered rings in the harness and were fasten-
ed there by pins. This carriage was called a car. The
collars used were made of twisted hay. A gentleman
who traded here at that time, says he has known eight
or ten of these cars to come out loaded in the morning
and, while their masters were taking their dram in
the store, the horses would get hungry and fall to eat-
ing up each other's collars. If one of the owners
happened to discover that his horse was losing his
collar, he would perhaps commence beating his neigh-
bor's horse; this would bring his master to the spot,
and he would resent the insult offered his horse by
laying it onto the man; soon all hands would be engaged in the melee, and it would end in a regular
turkey fight. After administering and receiving black
eyes and bloody noses sufficient to satisfy themselves,
they would call for more liquor, and this wonder
working beverage, which can make men cool in a hot
day, or warm in a cold one, had the same double
power of making men quarrelsome, or changing the
"lion to the lamb." After effecting a peace in this
way they would start for home the best of friends.

John Kempton built the first vessel at Oak Point;
she was called the Cynthia—115 tons. Capt. Grant
owned a small vessel called the Mamy Grant. Tobias
Oakman owned a sloop. In 1807 a vessel was built
by Andrews, Ware & Dean called the Orion—112 tons.
In 1806 a large ship of 700 tons burthen loaded with
timber for Liverpool opposite the Rankin place, (now
McGrath's.)

In 1806 Thorndike, Sears and Prescott, of Boston, having bought out the Ten Proprietors, came down here and made the first bargain with the settlers. Until now they had been squatters, they had settled upon a lot of land and commenced improvements without any permission. They offered the settlers the land for two dollars an acre, or offered to give half of their farms; if they would buy up the rest. Most of them preferred to purchase, and the first deeds were given in 1809.

After Prospect was set off, the town meetings were held in different buildings in this village until a school-house was built. Blaisdell's store, Sampson's store and McGlathry's stores were used at different times for this purpose; none of these buildings are now in existence. In 1805 the old school-house was built, located where Joseph Moody's house now stands.

Sometime during the early period of the settlement of this town, two boys in going to Mt. Ephraim, in Prospect, round Mt. Waldo, which was then an entire wilderness, lost their way in a snow storm and perished on the western side of the mountain, where they were afterwards found locked in each other's arms. From this circumstance the mountain received the name of Mt. Misery. In 1811 a large party of ladies and gentlemen from this village visited the mountain on horseback, and agreeing among themselves that the mountain deserved a better name, one of the company. (A. Jones, Esq.,) ascended a tree, broke a bottle and named it Mount Waldo. This name was selected on account of its being the highest land in the county of Waldo.

So late as this period the only riding carriage here was a chaise owned by Esquire McGlathry with square standing top; the first riding wagon was introduced sometime during the late war, those in first use were by no means such comfortable carriages as we have now; they had no springs, the body resting on the axle.

The year 1814 is memorable for the visit paid our river by a British fleet. It was in the month of September that the enemy took possession of Castine, and the same day the news of the event reached this place. It was expected that the enemy would immediately ascend the river with the intention of capturing the John Adams, an American frigate then lying at Hampden. To meet the emergency, the militia were called out, and a watch kept during the night. Soldiers were stationed as sentries at intervals along by the river, with orders to bring to all boats that might be ascending the river and inquire into their business. One boat belonging in Orrington containing three or four men, not answering when hailed, was fired upon; the shot fell into the water and did no harm. It had the effect however, of bringing them to and when their destination was known they were allowed to pass. The next morning the enemy's fleet was seen coming up the bay with a moderate breeze. Many of the people at the marsh had assembled on Beale Mt., from whence they looked down upon them with intense anxiety. As they came fanning along they kept boats out ahead to sound the way, sometimes using their barges manned by eighteen oars to tow their ships.

Sometime previous to this there had been brought into the river a vessel taken as a prize, loaded with cocoa, named the Kertusorf. Her valuable cargo had been sold at auction, being bid off by Boston gentlemen. One of the purchasers was Mr. Thorndike, one of the Ten Proprietors, who happened to be here. This cocoa was discharged into the McGlathry store and the vessel sent up river.

As soon as news was received that the British had captured Castine, and were expected up the river, teams were employed in removing the cocoa to Campbell's hill, where it was stored. They were actively engaged in the business that night and the next morning until the fleet was in the river, when it was thought prudent to desist, though it had not all been removed. During the night, Mr. Richard Thurston's store—the building now occupied by Mr. Wm. Holmes (the lot where Moody's cooper shop now stands) had been used as a place of rendezvous for the men employed as a watch during the night and the next morning as the fleet came along seeing armed men in the road by the store, they fired an eighteen lb. shot which passed through a window in the second story on the back side, came out of a window on the front side, passed through a shed attached to A. L. Kelly's house and struck the ground in McGlathry's field, not far from some females who had gone there for safety. This

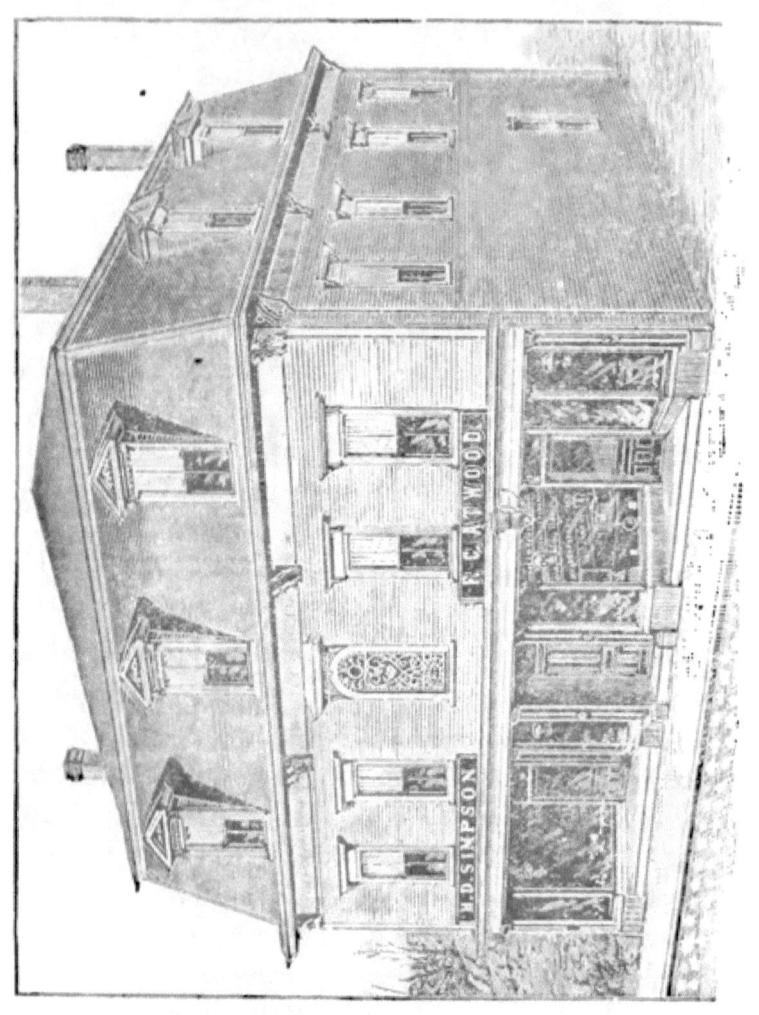

shot was intended to disperse the warlike demonstrations on the road, and it had the desired effect, for the soldiers scattered with great agility, being only impeded by tumbling over one another in their great anxiety to place themselves out of danger, and were soon lost sight of in the direction of the woods. It was now feared a regular cannonading would ensue, and the inhabitants began to seek places of safety for themselves. Perhaps the excitement which prevailed may be best shown by an anecdote. Those who lived upon Shaw's hill, fearing from their position that they were peculiarly exposed, collected their women and children and hurried them off in a body to the house now occupied by John Oakman (this house was back Northwest of the cemetery.) One gentleman who had got his blood very warm in the business and his mind abstracted in the excitement caught up a thin pair of pantaloons as he was leaving his house which he exchanged on the march for the thick ones he had on without being aware of it at the time or having any recollection of it afterwards; though of course so singular a proceeding did not pass unnoticed by the rest of the company.

No more shots were fired, and as the ships passed along they seemed desirious of exciting admiration rather than fear. On the decks the troops in rich uniform, were arranged so as to show to best advantage. The yards were covered with marines in uniform also, the fleet consisted of three large vessels, two of them sloops of war accompanied by smaller vessels, trans-

ports and gun boats, the whole making an imposing
and beautiful show, and only wanting to be divested
of the idea of war and bloodshed to call forth feelings
of admiration and delight.

The troops from the fleet were landed this side of
the Cove, where they made their encampment for the
night converting the neighboring houses into barracks.
The next morning a regiment of Militia of about seven
hundred men had been collected at Hampden, (most
of them had been under arms the day previous) and
were posted on the hill by the old meeting-house.
Capt. Morris, who commanded the frigate John Adams
lying at the wharf where he intrenched himself, intending to make a desperate resistance.   He also de-
tached his first lieutenant with an eighteen pounder
to assist the land force. This piece was planted in the
road by the meeting house and supported the right
wing of the infantry, the left extending in two lines
down towards the river.   A picket guard had been
stationed during the night on the road leading to the
Cove, to watch the movements of the enemy.   The
morning was very foggy which allowed the enemy to
advance upon the guard so closely that some of them
were taken prisoners at the lower corner.   One of the
prisoners was Tobias Oakman of this town.

As the British advanced they put their prisoners in
front of the column which is one of the expedients the
cruelty of war allows to defend themselves.   As they
ascended the hill after passing the bridge, the field-
piece opened its fire upon them, killing and wounding

several. This occasioned some confusion in their ranks, which the prisoners took advantage of to attempt their escape. Tobias Oakman, attempting this, was shot through the head and killed instantly, two others were more successful, one of the men ran behind a barn and got off, another fell down feigning death until the column passed over him, and then escaped.

Gen. Blake gave strict orders that no one should fire until they could see the enemy. The British on the contrary commenced a galling fire from behind a board fence which they had taken as a cover causing several in our ranks to fall. This our men could not stand, some here and there broke from the ranks and fled. This became more and more frequent, and soon the whole body was precipitately retreating in great confusion, amounting to a complete rout, some of them not having seen the enemy at all.

Capt. Morris, as soon as he knew the Americans were defeated spiked his guns, sent his men round a point of land in his boats to join the retreating soldiers remaining behind, himself to apply the match which blew up his vessel, thereby narrowly escaping being taken prisoner.

A knowledge of the facts in the case must lead to the conclusion that the defeat of Hampden was not as is generally supposed, disgraceful to our arms. In the first place it is never to be supposed that a body of men collected together with barely a day's notice, poorly equipped, without drill or discipline, officered

by men without practical knowledge, the men having
no confidence in their officers, nor the officers in their
men, can contend successfully with an equal body of
men who have been instructed in the necessary evolu-
tions for years, desperate men who have deliberate-
ly enlisted, commanded by officers who have made
war the study of their lives.   A case of successful
opposition under such circumstances is probably not
on record. The great mistake then, was in attempting
to resist at all unless a much larger and better drilled
army could have been collected.

Again the only chance of success was allowed to
pass, this was the night previous. Gen Herrick, who
was then commander of the cavalry, requested permission to go with a few hundred men and surprise
them in their encampment.   This request Gen. Blake
refused to grant.   Under cover of a dark, foggy night,
it might have been successful.

A mistake was made in occupying the brow of the
hill where our men could be seen by the enemy before
they themselves were visible on account of the fog.
No discredit can attach to the men composing our
force for they acted as all other men in the circumstances would have acted.   Much blame has been
attached to Gen. Blake and no doubt he erred greatly
in judgment, particularly in supposing that new militia
would stand a fire without breaking and not permitted
to return it; but the charges which have been alleged
against him of being bribed, and of cowardice, are not
sustained.   Those who knew him well say he was in-

capable of either. He was in the Revolutionary war; and was promoted to the rank of lieutenant for his bravery. At one time he, with a few men, captured some British officers who were at the time playing cards in a private house, and carried them into the American lines. He was afterwards Captain of a company, in the army raised under John Adams' administration, in apprehension of a war with France. At the time of the engagement at Hampden he lived at East Orrington, and was somewhat advanced in life. He has died within a few years aged more than 80, (this history was written in 1844.)

The enemy having possession of the place, committed many acts of wantoness in revenge for opposition they had met with, as breaking crockery, spilling molasses over the floors and mixing ashes with it, grinding up feather beds in a grist mill, etc., etc. It however relieves somewhat the dark page of history devoted to scenes of war, to record some deeds of humanity.

The wounded of our soldiers who could not be carried off the field in their hasty retreat fell into the hands of the enemy but were treated with great kindness, their wounds were dressed by their own surgeons and their wants well provided for. The wounded in all were thirteen, three of them from this town. John Carleton of this town, was shot down by a musket-ball in the thigh. He was partly carried off the field by his comrades, then dropped, he expostulated, but they answered we cannot help and left him to his fate while they sought their own safety by flight. He crawled

through a fence into a corn field, where he lay some
hours when he was found much exhausted by loss
of blood, by a British who gave him wine from his
canteen and removed him to a house where his wounds
were dressed.

In the morning before the action Solomon Tibbetts,
of this town, was going to join the ranks when he saw
a company marching on the street, which he took to
be a company sent out from the American lines to re-
connoitre.   They were dressed in a handsome uniform
with green jackets and high caps, and these were in
reality a German company composing the vanguard
of the British army.

He stood looking at them until they had got nearly
by him, when he heard one of them say, "there's an
enemy," with a pronunciation he knew was not Yankee,
then he started to run and as he passed them, the
whole company, twenty in number fired at him without
hitting him. The men then wanted to follow him with
the bayonet but the Captain said "No, let the poor
fellow live after running such a gauntlet as that."

The British fleet was up river six· or eight days
during which time they visited Bangor. On their way
back, they anchored off this place, took in water, and
made demand for provisions.   They were furnished
with ten oxen, about thirty sheep, potatoes and other
vegetables.   These were brought forward on the
assurance from the selectmen, that they should be
paid for by the town, but when a town meeting was
held, it was decided that the selectmen had transcend-

ed their powers and those who had furnished provisions had to bear their own loss. The Penobscot Indians followed the fleet down as far as this and camped on the opposite side of the river, expecting to be employed by the British in committing depredations, but here they were told that their services would not be required, and they returned home. Capt. Little was the greatest sufferer from the British here. He had a brig loaded with timber, which they took away with them and sent to Liverpool.

On their passage down the river, the sloop Sylph got aground on Haley's Point, (near the steam mill) where she discharged a quantity of cannon balls to lighten her. These were taken possession of by some of the people at the Marsh and were quite valuable.

Not long after the British had taken their departure, they sent up here a sloop under the protection of a flag of truce, demanding the cocoa which had been hauled into the country. That at first deposited at Campbell's Mills had been sent farther into the country. Some of it to Thorndike farm in Jackson, some was stored at Livermore's in Monroe, some at Lowe's in Goshen. They immediately commenced hauling it back, where Liet. Morse with about twenty armed soldiers, being routed at Eastport where he was stationed came through at Hampden. Hearing of this vessel he came down, went on board where he found a chest of arms which deprived her of the protection of a peace flag. He threw overboard the cocoa she had taken in, set the vessel on fire and cut her adrift. She floated up stream enveloped in flames, and soon burned to the water's edge. The Lieut. immediately took his departure carrying off her crew as prisoners. This bold act took our people by surprise, and filled them with great consternation. They feared the enemy would send a force and committ atrocities similar to those committed at Hampden. Many of the families moved into the back part of the town, and most sent off their household goods, losing half their crockery in transportation. Some barreled up their crockery and burned it in their gardens, many secured their silver spoons and other most valuable articles in this way. A deputation was immediately sent to Castine to state the facts concerning the burning of the vessel and to assure them that the people of this town had no part in the transaction. Upon first receiving information of it, Gen. Goslin ordered out six hundred troops which our commissioners took as a bad omen, but they succeeded in pacifying the Gen. and in satisfying him that our people were not to blame in the affair.

From the time the cocoa was first landed, the people generally seemed to regard it as lawful plunder, and few felt any compunctions in taking it wherever they could find it. When it was on the way to Campbell's a good many bags were filched from the carts, and after it was stored they would break into the buildings and steal it by night. Mr. Daniel Campbell had a quantity of it stored in his dwelling house, which for safe keeping, when the English officer was expected to demand it, he hid in the woods, every bag of which was carried off.

Sometimes a man would be riding along with a bag of it on his horse behind him, when another would come up, seize it, and make off in an opposite direction. One man from the back part of the town, stationed himself near the wharf as the teams came out loaded by night, and as they passed he would snatch a bag and hide it in a field of oats near where Edward Fernald's store is (now Mrs. A. E. Treat's.) In this way he had secured several bags and had gone for another when someone who had been watching him, carried off his booty, and he was obliged to go home without any cocoa. At the time the cocoa was thrown overboard from the vessel everybody there was welcome to all he could carry off, several boats were loaded; in one case they threw it into a boat until the owner begged them to stop, or they would sink him. When the vessel was burned, there were several loads on the road, which of course was supposed did not belong to any one in particular, and this scattered in all directions, while they were hauling the teamsters felt justified in taking their pay out of their loads, as they were not paid in any other way and one of them if no more, hauled his load to his own barn instead of the vessel and buried it in his hay-mow. After peace was declared, the owners in Boston sent down an agent to hunt up their cocoa, and search warrants were produced to seek for it. Some of it was recovered, but a great deal was never found; it was scattered in all possible ways. In some cases the floors were removed to make a safe deposit and replaced; one old lady outwitted the officer when he came by putting it in the pot over the fire. After the search was over it was offered very plentifully for sale. One man who had been very diligent, got a horse and peddled it round the country for six months. It found its way even to the Kennebec.

These facts are recorded because they are matters of history. It were to be wished for the credit of our town that they had never transpired; there were men, however, here, who would have nothing to do in the business, and who discountenanced all the proceedings altogether. The only excuse which can be offered to palliate such conduct, is that the cocoa was taken from the enemy, and would again fall into their hands, if not taken possession of. It is one of the thousand evils attending the dreadful scourge of war, the feeling of enmity and hostility blunts the moral sense and renders obtuse those faculties which under other circumstances would discriminate between right and wrong. That it was a thievish propensity alone that prompted these acts, is showed by the fact that Major Ware sent as many as fifty barrels of pickeled fish a mile or two back and had them rolled into a gully not far from the public road, where they remained scarcely depredated upon for sometime.

One other incident connected with this war deserves to be recorded in which some of the citizens of this town manifested great bravery. The Rertusorf which was taken with the cocoa, was brought in here by Capt.

Alexander Milliken of this place, who was put on board her as prize master. He afterwards commaned a Privateer fitted out at Thomaston which returned from her cruise without any success. Six of her crew three of them from this town, Isaac Milliken, Joseph Ellingwood, and Thomas Seavey, being dissatisfied with this result, went out in an open boat and captured a rich prize off Castine and carried her into Camden. This daring act was but poorly rewarded Justice should have given the prize to her captors, but the owners of the privateer by a protracted and expensive lawsuit succeeded in cutting them off with only their share as privateersmen.

✷ HISTORICAL SKETCHES. ✷

The Discovery of the Penobscot River.

By A. Jones, Esq.

Penobscot Bay and river were first discovered in 1605 by Capt. Geo. Weymouth from England with the ship Archangel who first made Monhegan, and thence sailing with his ship up on the west side of Long Island, as far as may be considered the head of the Bay, anchored his ship and with his boat, shallop as he called it, with seventeen men ascended the river proper, as he judged twenty miles. Capt. Weymouth considering the Bay on the east side of Long Island as part of a great river, says he passed up the river with a gentle breeze sixty miles from Penobscot harbor, as he named the first harbor he made. He said any man might conceive with what admiration they all consented. Many who had travelled in sundry countries and most famous rivers, affirmed them not to be comparable to this. He said he would not prefer it before England's richest treasure, the river Thames, but they all wished those excellent harbors, good depths, convenient breadths, and good holding ground, to be as well there as they found them here.—
He would boldly affirm it to be the most beautiful,

large and secure harboring river the world afforded, furnishing more good harbors for ships of all burdens than all England.

In 1629 a patent intended to embrace thirty miles in width on both sides of the Penobscot, was made to Beauchamp and Leverett in joint tenantry. As survivor Leverett became sole owner. By the laws of England, through the eldest sons, the whole patent was inherited by President Leverett of Harvard College, great grandson of the patentee.

President Leverett by deed divided the patent into ten shares, granting one share to a descendant of Gov. Bradford to extinguish some interfering claim, one to Spencer Phipps, son of Gov. Phipps who for a hat full of silver, had bought of Medarawando the Indian title and the other eight shares to his sons-in-law. In consideration of certain settling duties, those ten who had assumed the name of the Ten Proprietors, conveyed 100,000 acres including Camden, to a company that took the name of "The Twenty Associates."

As time advanced, danger arose that the title to the patent would be vacated for some defect. General Waldo was sent to England to get the patent confirmed. On a settlement with Waldo for advances and services the Ten Proprietors surrendered to him all their interest in the patent, reserving only 100,000 acres to be run out. About 1760 under Gov. Pownal, Gen. Waldo with a company of soldiers commenced building a fort at Fort Point. The father of Ebenezer Blaisdell of Frankfort, and the father of Samuel Jelli-

son, of Monroe, were two of the soldiers.   From an
accident that happened to him in a boat at a cape near
the fort the name of Jellison will go down to posterity.

While building the fort with a party of soldiers,
Jellison being of them, Waldo in a vessel sailed as far
up Penobscot river as he could, landed on the east
side, and at or near what is called Eddington Bend,
fixed in the earth a roll of sheet lead with inscriptions
claiming so far, as within his patent.   On his return
Waldo died suddenly, but not where he planted the
lead as tradition has it.   I am the more sure I had the
account correct from Jellison, on account of some
verses he repeated to me as made at the time by a wag.
Some of which I remember.   About Waldo he said:

> "There he lies, but how he fares
> Nobody knows, and nobody cares."

As to so much of the patent as fell east of the river,
one line was accidentally omitted in the description,
which left it so indefinite that no land was held on
that side.   In 1772, by one Chadwick as Surveyor,
100,000 acres were run out, marked and bounded for
the Ten Proprietors, bounded on the south by what is
now the south line of Frankfort extending north so as
to include all Hampden and much, perhaps all of
Bangor.   Next year the front lots were all marked off
fifty rods wide on the river, and a headline run aver-
ageing one mile from the river.

Except the wife of Gen. Knox and one of the name
of Waldo, all the heirs of Waldo were tories in the
Revolutionary war and left the country.   Their shares

were confiscated, and bought in by Gen. Knox.

After the war was over, on the application of Gen. Knox, his title was confirmed, and the limits of the Waldo patent defined, and settled in such a manner that more than half of the land that had been run out for the "Ten Proprietors" fell without the patent. To gain their assent and indemnify the "Ten Proprietors," Gen. Knox gave his bond; and having bought in some of the shares in that company, was elected to be clerk. After that the bond was never found. The end of the matter was, that under the ten grantees of President Leverett a tract intending to embrace thirty miles wide on both sides of Penobscot river, embraced only about 43,000 acres including what is now Frankfort and some of Swanville and Monroe.

Grand Jubilee at Winterport!

A WHOLE NIGHT DEVOTED TO REJOICING.

(From the Bangor Daily Evening Times,)
Tuesday, April 3, 1860.

On Wednesday evening, March 28, according to a
previous programme, the citizens of our new town,
with numerous invited friends and guests, celebrated
its birth.   During the day flags were set upon the
flag-staffs, and the shipping in port showed all their
bunting. Across Commercial street, in front of Clark's
hall, where the ball came off, a flag depended bearing
"WINTERPORT" on its tail end, and in front of the
Commercial House in the evening was a transparency,
"WINTERPORT, 1860."   In fact it was Winterport all
about town, and enthusiasm rose on tip-toe during
the day, and got upon stilts during the night.   Even
the dumb creation seemed conscious that something
more than usual was astir, and the very dogs, not less
than their masters, wagged their tails with joy.

With the approach of evening the citizens began to
assemble at the Commercial House, which was soon
filled.   It was brilliantly illuminated, and the count-
enances of the crowd beamed with smiles.   At the
same time, also, the dancers began to repair to Clark's
hall, which was in excellent order and handsomely
decorated, and connected with the hotel by an ample

walk, by which the convenience and comfort of the company, ebbing and flowing between the two great centres of attraction in waves of manly strength and female grace and beauty, were greatly facilitated. The company of dancers was large, embracing representations of all classes of citizens, and enticing into their whirl many who had never danced before.

The ladies were out in full force and in tasteful attire, with brows enwreathed with smiles for Winterport. The music, which was under the direction of P. C. Crane, of Frankfort, assisted by the Messrs. Ames, of Bucksport, and Mr. Geo. S. Silsby, of Winterport, was highly creditable to these artists. The managers, Messrs. Rich, Atwood and Fernald, of Winterport, and D. Fernald, of Frankfort, acquitted themselves in a manner worthy of all praise, and made the dance go merrily enough.

Meantime all was life and animation at the Commercial House, where the rooms were filled with a happy crowd, enjoying themselves in social conversation, plays, etc. At 12 o'clock supper was announced, when the capacity of mine host, Johnson, was never seen or tasted to better advantage, although he ever enjoyed a reputation second to no landlord for many miles around. Fowl, choice meats, fruits and confections of the choicest, and in profusion, were artistically and temptingly arrayed, and withstood the siege of hunger's great artillery from three fresh battalions of appreciating feeders, so great was the company present.

The festive exercises were also interspersed with speeches from Messrs. R. A. Rich, the Representative of Frankfort in the last Legislature, Otis Kaler, Esq., Hon. N. H. Hubbard, S. W. Merrill, Esq., of Frankfort, B. B. Thomas, Esq., Representative in the last Legislature from Newburg, who efficiently aided in the Winterport cause, and several others.

REMARKS OF R. A. RICH, ESQ.

Ladies and Gentlemen:—I am happy to see you this evening under such auspicious circumstances.

We have met to celebrate the consummation of an event which we have long ardently desired, and it is eminently proper that you should feel grateful for so favorable a termination of the struggle—grateful to your friends here and elsewhere, who, knowing your rights, dared to defend them. This result has been obtained by long continued and persistent effort. It has cost many hard days' work, many sleepless nights, as well as much money. But it is at last accomplished, and we meet to celebrate the incorporation of the town of Winterport. In my efforts the past winter, I labored to promote, as I believed, the interest of Frankfort as well as of Winterport. But perhaps the citizens of Frankfort are not prepared to appreciate my labors as you do this evening. But I believe the time will come when they will rise up and call those blessed that have been instrumental in severing the ties that bound us together. We have not accomplished all that we desired. We were loth to part company with some in the old town of Frankfort,

nd we now say to them, that we hope the time is not
ir distant when we shall be permitted to extend to
iem a brother's hand and a brother's welcome within
ie limits of Winterport. I am pleased to see some of
iem with us this evening, and in the name of this
ompany, I bid them welcome, and in conclusion I
ill give you the following:

THE FRIENDS OF WINTERPORT—They can manifest
ieir interest in her welfare in no better way than by
:udying to promote harmony among all her citizens.

REMARKS BY OTIS KALER.

Ladies and Gentlemen:—We have met together this
vening to celebrate the organization of the town of
Vinterport. Many of us enlisted in this enterprise
ome ten years since. In 1851 a petition was present-
l to the Legislature praying for the same line that
e petitioned for this year, as well as last, but the
egislature, or I should have said the Senate, saw fit
) give us this line, and sever our village. Still we
:el thankful for a part, feeling that to be the way to
et more. We have thus far succeeded in our endeavors,
nd feel to rejoice in our success, which is demonstrated
y the gathering here this evening. While we surround
iis festal board, with hearts overflowing with grati-
ide, we should not forget our friends in the lower
art of the village, who are separated from us by this
ne. They have labored shoulder to shoulder with
s, to bring about a division of the town, hoping
ereby to save it from bankruptcy, but they remain
i Frankfort still, to be goaded a time longer; and

while we feel to rejoice, a very different feeling pervades
their hearts. No doubt they feel gratified that a portion
are free; but still many of them feel sad at the thought
that a town line should separate them from their
friends.   But they have everything to hope for in the
future. The annexation of this village must be effected
at no distant day.   But I am admonished that I must
be brief, as there are others who are waiting to partake
of the bounties of mine host, and will close with the
following:

OUR FRIENDS. IN THE LOWER VILLAGE, WHO ARE
SEPARATED BY THE TOWN LINE—May their watch-word
be annexation; and may they never cease to echo it,
until they shall accomplish their purpose.

Mr. Merrill, of Frankfort, returned his heartfelt
thanks for the kind and warm reception which had
welcomed him and other friends from Frankfort, and
gave the following sentiment:

WINTERPORT—May her citizens always live in perfect harmony, and may her soil be en*Riched* by her
peace loving citizens; and may it bring forth, year
after year, something better than *Chick*-weed.

This sentiment was followed by three cheers for
Frankfort.

We regret that we were called away, and lost the
remarks of Hon. N. H. Hubbard, B. B. Thomas,
and others.

Letters were also read, in response to invitations,
from Hon. Josiah H. Drummond, of Waterville.
Senator in the last Legislature, M. R. Ludwig, of

Thomaston, H. G. Cole, of Manchester, and Timothy Rowell, of Vassalboro, Representatives in the same, J. A. Peters, of Bangor, and others, all expressing their best wishes for the prosperity of the new town.

At 3 o'clock A. M., Thursday, the few sleepers of Winterport were aroused by the firing of a grand salute and the ringing of bells, whose echoes probably broke in upon the slumbers of the neighboring towns.

At 5 o'clock, "night's candles" and the kerosene at Clark's hall having burnt out together, the weary-legged dancers repaired to the hotel to engage in the remaining amusements, which were terminated by a refreshing breakfast for such whose enthusiasm and strength lasted till that hour. Thus ended the celebration of Winterport's inauguration, which all who participated in it will long remember as the event of a lifetime.

The Vexed Question Settled.

(PROGRESSIVE AGE, March 29, 1872.)

Differences having existed between the two tribes dwelling on the Passagassawaukeag river, and that part of the Penobscot above the "narrers" known as Winterport, as to the superiority of their respective ports in the winter season, also as to their rights and privileges touching clams and tom-cods, it was resolved in the general council of the Winterport tribe, that a delegation of their chief men should be sent to the "Waukeag" tribe with a proposition to form with the chief men of that tribe, a Joint High Commission to settle all matters in dispute. The following chiefs were accordingly appointed:

HAM-CU-SHAN,—Sec'y of the Interior.

FATWOOD,—Com. of Agriculture.

VILLIAM-DE-LA-WAY,—Com. on Interior Waters.

EC-A-RYE,—Lord Mayor.

BEN-JAM-TOMSON,—Lord High Admiral.

LOUIS-HAILIE,—Capt. Horse Marines.

A-EFURNELL,—Sec'y of War.

AITCH-Z-CHAPMUN,—G. H. Steward.

TOEBEE-HOLT,—Chief Police.

TOOT-KRAIN,—Dep.   "

JHON-FATWOOD,—Heir-apparent.

JHOE-KLEARK,—Lord H. K. of the Seal.

Sledges were immediately got in readiness, and, on Tuesday, the distinguished Commissioners set out on their journey. On their leaving, a dispatch was sent, appropriately directed to the chief marshal of the Waukeag tribe, advising him of the fact, and bespeaking for them a hospitable welcome. He was apprised that, in consequence of no arrivals from the warmer regions, the tribe were short of supplies, and the "inards" of the Commissioners would need nourishment. That as their most natural food was blubber meat, a large supply of that would be necessary. He was further urged to provide for their *spiritual* wants, which would undoubtedly be great. On their way the commissioners tarried for a short time at the chief village of a small but spunky tribe, the Nathan-Barnabas tribe. They were received with high honor. Flags heralded their coming, and the chiefs received them warmly, treating them on cider juice in the original packages. On their arrival at "Waukeag," the first care was to visit the steamer Cambridge to ascertain whether the Winterport supplies on board were not suffering evaporation; they having "hearn" that frequent parties of the "Waukeags" had been seen on board, in the night time, in a hilarious mood. They however found Capt. Johnson keeping a sharp lookout for Winterport interests. Making a hasty examination of the Winterport portion of the cargo, they were gratified to find that it had not deteriorated either in *quantity or strength.* Turning their sledges, they proceeded to the American House, in and around which a large number of "Waukeags" had congregated. As their sledges arrived in front, loud cheers of welcome rent the air. Their appearance was somewhat grotesque. Their manner of dress bespoke them as natives of a cold region; huge over garments made of the skins of the seal and polar bear; immense caps of fantastic shape encircled their heads; their faces were nearly concealed by heavy mustaches, and huge moccasins were worn upon their feet. Their sledges were of curious make; the runners were a prolongation of the thills; into them were mortised rude studs surmounted by cross bars, and upon these were placed seated tops. One had a portion of the top of the old "one hoss shay;" another had the unpainted top of a half-moon sleigh, which one of the oldest men of the tribe commenced to build, upwards of a half century ago, but never made the bottom. The runners of these sledges were of a native wood called hornbeam. The harnesses of the animals were evidently extemporized. From the thill of one sled a single, large, old-fashioned bell depended, and from another a cowbell.

A board of Commissioners on the part of the "Waukeags" was at once selected, and the Joint Commission was formed. Apartments for the sittings were provided by landlord Robbins with the necessary supply of *ice-water,* and he hastened to prepare blubber-meat. The first point considered by the commissioners was ice;

first as a hygenic agent applied outwardly and inwardly, especially *inwardly* under proper medical restric-
tions, obtainable at the town Agencies; and, second,
as a product of our "Enchanted Land" and the
following propositions were finally agreed upon:

1st. That ice is a blessing to our tribes, and its
use, especially on 4th of July occasions, is indispensable; that as a product, it is of great value to our
state; that merely on account of its interfering tempo-
rarily with the free navigation of our Penobscot bay
and harbors it should not be denounced as a nuisance,
but should rather be regarded as a token of good; and
that all disrespectful allusions to it should hereafter
be discountenanced.

2d. That our respective ports or harbors are not riv-
als; that while a constant open harbor at Winterport
is essential not only to the happiness of that tribe, but
also to the happiness and prosperity of the No-rum-be-
gar tribe, *alias* "poor Bangor," a constant open port
at "Waukeag" is not less essential to the happiness
of that tribe and to the convenience of certain interior
tribes, known as the Somerset and Piscataquis tribes,
(the latter of which in the recent legislature expressed
its longing desire to reach said open port;) and that
in future, no speeches, dispatches, or editorials tending
to draw unfavorable comparisons between the two
ports, ought to be regarded with favor.

3d. That clams and tom-cods are strictly local in-
stitutions, and that the members of the respective
tribes have, under our ger-lori-ous constitution, the

right to manage and dispose of them according to the per-inci-ples of "Squatter Sovereignty," and that all further agitation concerning them should cease.

Done at "Waukeag" the 26th day of March, Anno Domingo, 1872.

Signed, &c.

Upon the conclusion of the above arduous labors, the High Commission was informed that blubber-meat was ready, and they forthwith repaired to the refreshment room; and after satisfying their delicate appetites, and indulging in pleasant sallies of wit, also of wisdom, they separated to submit their "doin's" to their respective tribes.

THE LEVEE.

(From The Volunteer, March 12, 1863.)

The ladies of Winterport and Frankfort have a wide
and well deserved reputation for good works. At the
call of duty they always respond cheerfully and ener-
getically.

It was, therefore, to be expected of them, that the
necessities of our gallant soldiers should awaken their
profound solicitude, and induce them to renewed ac-
tivity in all projects for their relief. These expecta-
tions were more than realized in the Levee in aid of
the Sanitary Commission, held at Fernald's Hall,
Frankfort, on the evening of the 18th and 19th ult.
which was remarkably well attended, and a success
socially and financially.

The hall, under the tasty and dextrous manipulation
of the decorative committee, S. W. Merrill, Capts.
Geo. L. Havener and Chas. Grant, assisted by a score
of our prettiest young ladies, fairly bloomed with
elegance and beauty.

The entrance to the hall was appropriately festooned
with National flags. Entering, the eye first rests upon
the twin sentiments of Justice, "Liberty and Union" in
evergreen letters, charmingly draped with flags, and
ornamented with beautiful wreaths, uniquely made of
parched corn, prettily trimmed with the "red white,

and blue," contributed by Miss L. C. Cushing, whose taste and ingenuity in such ornamental matters is unrivaled.

By a graceful combination of flags over and around the speakers' stand the effect was very striking and harmonius.

A large portrait of Washington, decked with minature flags, overlooked with paternal dignity the happy throng, seeming to rest the benign blessing upon the enterprise. Over the portrait in semi-circular letters of evergreen, was the appropriate appeal,—" *Lid the Soldiers.*"

At the right of the dais was the veteran Gen. Scott in portrait, represented in his more vigorous youth, and on the left a picture representing the "Capture of Maj. Andre" set a striking lesson of incorruptible patriotism, especially forcible in these days of perjury and treason.

The other extreme of the hall was draped "Big Flag" —the "Old Eagle" as ferociously defiant, as when through many a stormy political campaign, he breasted the tide of treason just then in its flood setting in upon us. Several historic national pictures were blended with the decorations; and from the center of the hall a tastefully decorated chandelier was suspended from which was festooned to each end, the national pennant. The whole, by common consent acknowledged never to have been excelled on any previous similar occasion.

The higher sentiments of the soul having been by

hese "strange devices" brought into harmony with
he objects sought, it was natural that that which
'ministers to the body as well as the soul" should
possess *absorbing* interest. The tables! how could we
neglect them so long! and what shall we say of them!
They were patriotically jubilant with the rich abundance heaped so liberally upon them; they ached with
joyous plates and platters of animal food, and were
"tickled almost to death" with luscious fruits and
choice "*bon-bons.*"

Here men of iron muscle might stock themselves
with material for deeds of mighty valor; and there
might be seen delicasies which would deliciously
agitate the palate of the favorite of the harem. Such
a tabular testimonial of feminine grace and beauty
would honor a more pretentious community than ours.

The entertainment was introduced by a few excellent
remarks by Hon. T. Cushing, detailing the mission of
the Sanitary Commission, and defending it from the
aspersions upon it of semi-secessionists, and luke warm
unionists. Rev. Mr. Small continued by reading letters
from the Army eulogizing the Commission, and ex-
tolling its efforts.

Mrs. Carrie Chase then sang the "Star Spangled
Banner" with spirit and good taste; a select choir
under the leadership of that veteran vocalist, B. B.
Cushing, Esq., joining in the chorus with grand and
stirring effect.

Miss Lizzie Varney, of Bangor, who had kindly
consented to aid the entertainment, was then present-

ed by Mr. T. H. Cushing, and read the following
poetic gem:

THE MOTHERS OF 1862.

They call for "able-bodied men."
    Now there's our Roger, strong and stout;
He'd beat his comrades out and out
    In feats of strength and skill—what then?

What then?—why only this: you see
    He's made of just that sort of stuff
They want on battle-fields; enough!
    What choice was left for him and me?

So, when he asked me yesterweek,
    "Your blessing, mother!" did I heed
The great sob at my heart, or need
    Another word that he should speak?

Should I sit down and mope and croon,
    And hug my selfishness, and cry
"Not *him*, my first-born!" no, not I!
    Thank heaven I pipe a nobler tune.

And yet I love him like my life,
    This stalwart, handsome lad of mine!
I warrant me, he'll take the shine
    Off half who follow drum and fife!

Now God forgive me, how I prate!
    Ah, but the *mother* will leap out
Whatever folds we wrap about
    Our foolish hearts, or soon or late.

No doubt 'tis weakness—mother-lip
    Extolling its own flesh and blood;
A trick of weakly womanhood
    That we should scourge with thong and whip;

No doubt—and yet I should not dare
    Lay an unloved, cheap offering
Upon my country's shrine, nor bring
    Aught but was noble, sweet and fair.

And so I bring my boy,—too glad
    That he is worthy, and that I,
Who bore him once in agony,
    Such glorious recompense have had.

Take him, my country! he is true
    And brave and good; his deeds shall tell
More than my foolish words 'tis well!
    God's love be with the lad and you.

God's love and care—and when he comes
    Back from the war, and through the street
The crazy people flock to meet
    My hero, with great shouts, and drums,

And silver trumpets braying loud,
    And silken banners starry-gay,
'Twill be to me no prouder day
    Than this; nay, nay nor half so proud.

And if—God help me—if, instead,
    They flash this word from some red field:
"His brave, sweet soul, that would not yield,
    Leaped upward, and they wrote him 'dead'"—
I'll turn my white face to the wall,
    And bear my grief as best I may
For Roger's sake and only say
    "He knoweth best who knoweth all."

And when the neighbors come to weep,
    Saying, "alas, the bitter blow!"
I'll answer, nay, dear friends, not so!
    Better my Roger's hero-sleep.

And nobler far such lot, than his
    Who dare not strike with heart and hand
For freedom and dear fatherland
    Where death's dark missiles crash and whiz.

> And Roger's mother has no tear
>> So bitter as her tears would be
> If from the battles of the free,
>> Her son shrank back with craven fear.

The patriotic struggles of the mother's soul with love of country and her boy; and the eloquent pathos, so beautifully expressed by the poetess, were thoroughly appreciated by Miss Varney, and ably rendered. The profound attention of the audience, with visible emotion manifested by mothers whose sons had craved the farewell blessing, were fitting tributes to the emotional power of the reader.

The "Red, White and Blue" was sung by Miss Louise Morgan; Mrs. Carrie Chase presided at the piano. Rev. Mr. Jewell followed with excellent remarks, recommending the Christian Commission to public sympathy, and presented its scope and mission in an interesting and able manner.

A grand choral anthem was given—"Our Land of Liberty," solo by B. B. Cushing, Esq. Mr. Cushing seemed to throw into its execution the ardor and spirit of his younger days and never sang better.

At this point, in response to a vigorous appeal from the chairman, a general attack in front, flank and rear, upon the edibles was made by the combined forces of old and young.

The smoking stews, the fragrant chowder, and the stoical ice cream, yielded rapidly to the appetizing influences brought into action against them, while barricades of pies and tarts and other "fine arts" went

...n suddenly before the gastronomic attacks of the
...orous young patriots. Amiability and sociability
...d the hour and "all went merry as the marriage
...l."

...t a late hour the entertainment concluded for the
...ning by some excellent and mirth provoking sing-
...and playing by Mr. Geo. Coffin.

...he elements conspired against the Levee the second
...ning, but only added to the sociability of the crowd
...ch assembled, regardless of mud and water.

... A. Rich, Esq. "opened the ball" with some
...racteristic remarks, and the choir gave some
...ndid singing; indeed, the musical treat was *the*
...ure of the evening. The staunch "Old Star
...ngled Banner," "National Hymn," "Sacred
...hem." "National Prayer,"—solo by Miss Morgan
...ll finely executed.

...eo. S. Silsby, the model post-master of the county,
...Miss Clara Dudley, musical instructor of Hampden
...demy, sang a beautiful duet entitled "Heavenly
...me." The spirit of the composition and character
...he music was admirably adapted to the superior
...or of Mr. Silsby and the sweet and highly culti-
...ed voice of Miss Dudley. The exercises closed by
...song, solo by Geo. Coffin, the audience joining in
...chorus, and other selections ranging from grave to
..., by the same gentleman.

...reat credit is due the ladies for the manner in which
...entertainment was originated and executed. Where
...acquitted themselves so well, it may seem invidious

to particularize, but we cannot refrain from acknowl
edging the personal efforts of Mesdames Otis Kaler
T. Cushing, P. Cushing, J. Lord, P. Powers, Carrie
Houston, True, Geo. Fernald, Gerry and Miss Sarah
Abbott.

We should do injustice to the indefatigable Wetmore
the prompt and active Gerry, and the tireless Master
George Merrill, if we failed to mention the very im
portant and almost indispensable services rendered by
them to the Levee.

The construction Com., Messrs. Ammi Merrill and
Peter Cushing, performed their duties with skill and
promptness.

Nearly half a peck of No. 1 shin plasters testified
to the efficiency of that financial autocrat, J. Lord
No "promises to pay in even dollars," of doubtful
convertibility, lodged in his exchequer.

Mrs. J. Lord presided over the culinary department
which is only another way of saying that the "stews"
were at least 75 per cent above par.

As we have once said, the whole affair was a success
and very creditable to all engaged in it.

Gala Day at Winterport.

THE NEW HALL OF GARFIELD LODGE OF ODD FELLOWS DEDICATED.

Thursday, December 13, 1894, was a gala day at Vinterport. The beautiful hall of Garfield Lodge of Odd Fellows, (see cut on page 16) was publicly dedicated by the Grand Lodge of Maine.

The weather was not favorable, but it did not deter large crowd from attending. At noon a large deleation of Odd Fellows and Rebekahs went up from ucksport on the steamer Bismark. A dozen or more rove up from Belfast and Bangor furnished its quota.

At one o'clock the street procession moved, lead by 1e Winterport band. The line was composed of lodges 1 Winterport and Bucksport, the visitors from other laces joining the ranks of these two lodges. The rand Lodge of Maine brought up at the rear. The 1arch was made through the principal streets.

At 3 o'clock the lodge room was filled to overflowing y the citizens and visitors. The beautiful ceremony f dedication was handsomely performed by Grand 1aster Samuel Adams, of Belfast, assisted by N. G. ettingill, as Grand Warden. Rev. J. P. Simonton, f Winterport, as Grand Chaplain, R. G. Dyer as

Grand Marshal, W. K. Keene, Grand Herald of the North, Dr. Baker, of Winterport, Grand Herald of the South, C. R. Coombs, Grand Herald of the East, and B. B. Greenlaw, Grand Herald of the West. All the officers excepting those specified, belonged in Belfast. The music furnished was of a high order.

Grand Master Adams delivered an appropriate address, which was well received.

At the close of the dedicatory ceremony, the entire company repaired to the dining-room of Union Hall where an excellent supper was served by the members of Garfield Lodge. The ceremonies of the day closed with a ball at Union Hall.

Garfield Lodge, No. 99, was instituted Feb. 7, 1883, with six charter members. It now numbers nearly 200. The present year it has built a handsome block on Main street which it owns. The first floor contains two large stores, the second floor two offices and a banquet room.

The third floor contains the lodge room and ante rooms. The hall is tastily furnished, and Garfield Lodge is to be congratulated upon its fine home. The lodge is among the first in the state.

When Garfield Lodge undertakes a thing they never leave it half done. Everything was first-class and the several committees performed their work in proper style. P. C. Rich was Chief Marshal of the day, assisted by G. H. Dunton and A. W. Shaw. Geo. F. Snow was marshal of the home lodge. Longee's Orchestra, of Bangor, appeared on the stage at 8 P. M.,

full dress and gave the party a great treat, discours-
g the finest music that ever came from this stage.
he orchestra consisted of five pieces and every part
as skillfully performed and with that harmony which
akes friendship and love truly satisfying, every
ember of the party reciprocated by perfect order and
ords of praise. The order of dances was well arranged
id carried out to a letter. On the front of the folder
ere emblems of the order and the printing was done
scarlet and blue. The badges also represented the
olor of the degrees. The quartette deserves much
aise for their services, as every number was well
ndered. The parts were as follows:

Mrs. C. R. Lougee, Soprano; Miss Chase, Contralto;
r. Haley, Tenor; Mr. Howland, Bass.

Winterport, Me., July 12, 1897.

Dear Sir:—

I understand you intend to publish a history of Frankfort (now Winterport.)   I thought it might interest you and your readers to know something of one of the old pioneers and early settlers of Frankfort. I take the liberty to tell you how he gave away to his children all of the great tract of land he bought of the original proprietors.

My grandfather, Ebenezer Blaisdell, was a soldier under Gen. Waldo, and helped build a fort at Fort Point about the year 1760 which was afterwards destroyed by the British.   In going up and down the river with Gen. Waldo he became acquainted with the location of the land which he afterwards bought and settled on.   He built a house on this land in 1785, being the third frame house built in the town, which would make it 112 years old, and is now the oldest house in town, and is now owned and occupied by E. F. Blaisdell.   This tract of land run from the river back, one mile, and from the side lane near the Abbott watering-trough, to the farm now owned by John M. Snow. Quite a number of years before he died he gave all of this land to his children.

He gave six acres on the river to his son, Ebenezer Blaisdell, Jr.   The next lot he gave to his daughter, Mrs. Grant, where Mrs. Thos. McDonough now lives. Next to this lot he gave a lot to his daughter, Mrs. Dunning, where James Jepson now lives.   The next lot, where the Sproul barn now stands and across the

1 where Mr. Wm. B. Sproul now lives, he gave to
daughter, Mrs. Fernald.   The next lot, where the
ll house now stands, he gave to his daughter, Mrs.
ey. The next lot, where the old house now stands,
t by him in 1785, he gave to his son, Ebenezer.
: next lot he gave to his daughter, Mrs. McIntire.
:re is no building on this lot. The next lot he gave
is daughter, Mrs. Chick, where Miss Jennie Chick
· lives.   Next lot he gave to his daughter, Mrs.
ming, and is now owned by T. H. Sproul.   The
t lot of three acres where the Catholic church now
ids, he gave to his son, William.   The next lot,
:re Capt. Dudley now lives, together with all the
 of the original tract, he gave to his son. James,
ake care of him and his wife during their lives.
ies afterwards exchanged farms with Capt. Childs,
'emiquid, Bristol, where he moved, taking his fath-
nd mother with him, where they died. The most of
 land given to his son. James, is now owned by
Dudley heirs.

Yours truly,

E. F. BLAISDELL.

THE END.